Dear Parent:

Your child's love of reading starts here!

Every child learns to read in a different way and at his or her own speed. Some go back and forth between reading levels and read favorite books again and again. Others read through each level in order. You can help your young reader improve and become more confident by encouraging his or her own interests and abilities. From books your child reads with you to the first books he or she reads alone, there are I Can Read Books for every stage of reading:

SHARED READING
Basic language, word repetition, and whimsical illustrations, ideal for sharing with your emergent reader

BEGINNING READING
Short sentences, familiar words, and simple concepts for children eager to read on their own

READING WITH HELP
Engaging stories, longer sentences, and language play for developing readers

READING ALONE
Complex plots, challenging vocabulary, and high-interest topics for the independent reader

I Can Read Books have introduced children to the joy of reading since 1957. Featuring award-winning authors and illustrators and a fabulous cast of beloved characters, I Can Read Books set the standard for beginning readers.

A lifetime of discovery begins with the magical words **"I Can Read!"**

Visit www.icanread.com for information
on enriching your child's reading experience.

Pete the Kitty Goes to the Doctor
Art copyright © 2019 by James Dean
Text copyright © 2019 by Kimberly and James Dean
Pete the Kitty © 2015 Pete the Cat, LLC
Pete the Kitty is a registered trademark of Pete the Cat, LLC, Registration Number 5576697
All rights reserved. Printed in the United States of America.
No part of this book may be used or reproduced in any manner whatsoever without written permission except in the case of brief quotations embodied in critical articles and reviews. For information address HarperCollins Children's Books, a division of HarperCollins Publishers, 195 Broadway, New York, NY 10007.
www.icanread.com

Library of Congress Control Number: 2019937385
ISBN 978-0-06-286833-6 (trade bdg.) —ISBN 978-0-06-286832-9 (pbk.)

Typography by Chrisila Maida
20 21 22 23 LSCC 10 9 8 7 6 5

❖

First Edition

Pete the Kitty GOES TO THE DOCTOR

by Kimberly & James Dean

HARPER

An Imprint of HarperCollinsPublishers

Pete the Kitty wakes up.

It is time to go to school.

Pete stretches his arms.
He stretches his legs.

Ouch! Pete's belly hurts.

Pete calls his dad.
"My belly does not
feel groovy," he says.

Pete's dad feels his head.
"You do not have a fever,"
Dad says.
"You just need some rest."

Dad tucks Pete
back into his bed.
Dad kisses Pete's head.

Pete pulls up his covers.
He thinks he will have
a cool day at home.

Pete starts to play
with his trains.

Then Pete starts to paint
a picture.

"It is time to get dressed,"
Dad says.

"It is time to go
to the doctor."

Pete does not want to go
to the doctor.
Pete is scared of the doctor.

Dad says,

"The doctor is cool.

She is not scary."

Dad takes Pete
to the doctor's office.
They wait their turn.

The waiting room is fun.
Pete gets to play with
lots of far-out toys.

The nurse comes for Pete.
She takes him
to another room.

The nurse checks
for a fever.

The doctor comes in.
She checks Pete's ears.

She checks Pete's eyes.

The doctor feels Pete's belly.

She listens to Pete's heart.
The doctor even lets Pete
listen to her heart.

"Don't worry,"
the doctor says.
"It is just a bellyache."

The doctor gives Pete
a cool sticker.
She tells Pete to rest.

Dad takes Pete home.

Dad lets Pete rest in bed.

Pete will feel better soon.

Dad was right.

The doctor was not scary.

She was nice.

Pete feels better.

Soon he will be back to

his groovy self again!